For Nat, of course! G.A.

For Nick Fantastic,
with lots of love   K.M.

ORCHARD BOOKS
338 Euston Road, London NW1 3BH
Orchard Books Australia
Level 17/207, Kent Street, Sydney, NSW 2000

First published by Orchard Books in 2008

A CIP catalogue record of this book
is available from the British Library.

ISBN: 978 1 84121 488 7
10 9 8 7 6 5 4 3 2 1

Printed in China

Orchard Books is a division of Hachette Children's Books,
an Hachette Livre UK company.
www.hachettelivre.co.uk

NAT FANTASTIC

Giles Andreae

Katharine McEwen

ORCHARD BOOKS

This is Nat. His mummy is about to read him a story.
Nat loves nothing more than being read to at bedtime
for reasons which will soon become clear.

"Hello, darling," said his mummy.
"What story shall we have tonight then?"

"Let's have this," said Nat, picking
out one of his all-time favourites.
He cuddled up to his mummy
and she began to read.

"Oh goodness!" said Nat's mummy
after a little while.

"I think I've left the carrots on!
I'll just pop downstairs and
turn them off . . .

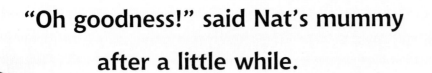

I won't be long!"

As soon as she went out of his bedroom
Nat's nose began to tingle. The tingle grew
tinglier and tinglier until . . .

"AAACHOOOO!"

Nat sneezed an almighty sneeze.

FLASH!

BANG!

And it was true. That sneeze had changed Nat into a miniature superhero!

Suddenly Nat felt himself whizzing through the air at a million miles an hour in his amazing silver pyjamas.

Then **SPLASH!** he landed in the middle of a rushing river in Africa. It was very lucky that he landed in that particular river because . . .

as soon as he looked around he spotted a boat full of little girls with a huge crocodile heading towards them, greedily licking its lips.

Straight away
Nat Fantastic grabbed
the crocodile round
its tummy.

OOF

He wrestled and rolled
and rumbled with it
for ages, splashing
around like mad until . . .

BIFF

OOYA

finally the crocodile gave up.

"You're just too strong for me,
Nat Fantastic," it said, and it swam
back exhausted to the riverbank.

"You're amazing, Nat Fantastic!" the girls all said.
"You saved our lives!" And they cuddled and kissed
him for ages, which Nat quite liked.

Suddenly Nat felt his nose begin to tingle again.

It got tinglier and tinglier until . . .

"AAACHOOOO!"

Nat sneezed an almighty sneeze, and he was back in bed.

At that very moment Nat's mummy
came into his room.
"Sorry, darling," she said. "Now where
were we?" She picked up the book
again and began to read.

After a little while more the
telephone started to ring.

Ring!

Ring! Ring!

Ring!

"Oh, do you mind if
I answer that, sweetheart?
I'll be back in just a second . . ."

Immediately Nat's nose began
to tingle. The tingle grew tinglier
and tinglier until . . .
"AAACHOOOO!"
Nat sneezed an almighty sneeze.

FLASH!

BANG!

NAT FANTASTIC'S IN THE ROOM!

Suddenly Nat felt himself whizzing through the air at a million miles an hour in his amazing silver pyjamas.

Then **BUMP!**

he landed in the middle of an old lady's garden.

It was very lucky that he landed in that particular garden because the old lady's house had just been struck by a great bolt of lightning, and it was quickly falling down. "Help! Help!" shrieked the old lady.

HELP!

Straight away Nat Fantastic got an enormous ladder and climbed up it with a huge box of tools.

He hammered
and sawed . . .

and nailed
and glued . . .

and fixed . . .

and screwed the whole house back together again.

When Nat got back to the ground
the old lady gave him a huge kiss,
which Nat was only quite keen on,
and an enormous bag of sweets,
which he was very
keen on indeed.

Suddenly Nat felt his nose begin to tingle again.

It got tinglier and tinglier until . . .

"AAACHOOOO!"

Nat sneezed an almighty sneeze, and he was back in bed.

At that very moment Nat's mummy
came into his room.
"Sorry, darling," she said. "Now where were we?"
She picked up the book again
and began to read.

After a little while more the doorbell rang. **BUZZZZZZ!**
"Oh, sweetheart, I'd better just see who that is,"
said Nat's mummy. "I really won't be a minute."

Immediately Nat's nose began
to tingle. The tingle grew tinglier
and tinglier until . . .

"AAACHOOOO!"

Nat sneezed an almighty sneeze.

FLASH!

BANG!

WHIZZ!

KABOOM!

NAT FANTASTIC'S
IN THE ROOM!

Suddenly Nat felt himself whizzing

through the air at a million miles an

hour in his amazing silver pyjamas.

Then **BOUNCE!**
he landed right
outside a
huge building.

It was very lucky that he landed right outside that
particular building because it happened to be a bank . . .

and right at that particular moment some naughty bank robbers were running away with huge sacks of money.

NK

"Stop thief! Stop thief!"
the bank manager was shouting.

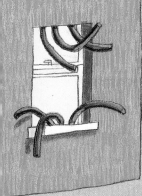

Straight away Nat Fantastic raced after the bank robbers.

They were very fast runners . . .

but Nat Fantastic was even faster.

He soon caught up with them
and wrestled them to the ground.

In no time at all Nat Fantastic had them
tied up with a big rope, and he handed
the huge sacks of money back
to the bank manager.

The bank manager was very pleased
indeed, and he gave Nat one of the
sacks of money to say thank you.

Suddenly Nat felt his nose
begin to tingle again.

It got tinglier and tinglier until . . .

"AAACHOOOO!"

Nat sneezed an almighty sneeze,
and he was back in bed.

At that very moment Nat's mummy
came into his room.
"Sorry, darling," she said.
"Now where were we?"
She picked up the book again
and began to read.

This time Nat's mummy
read right to the end
of the book.

She tucked Nat into his bed and gave him
a goodnight kiss and a lovely big hug.
"I love you, sweetheart," she said, as she
tiptoed softly out of his bedroom.

Nat smiled and laid his head down
on the pillow.

But guess what . . .?

Just as Nat was beginning to drift off
to sleep he felt his nose begin to tingle!
Oh no, Nat! Don't sneeze! Not now, Nat!

DON'T SNEEZE!

NO!!!

"AAACHOOOO!"